双语名著无障碍阅读丛书

经典集锦

# 新月集

## The Crescent Moon

[印度] 泰戈尔 著

郑振铎 译

中国出版集团

中译出版社

**图书在版编目(CIP)数据**

新月集：英汉对照/(印)泰戈尔著；郑振铎译. —北京：中译出版社，2017.6（2018.4 重印）

（双语名著无障碍阅读丛书）

ISBN 978-7-5001-5278-1

Ⅰ.①新…　Ⅱ.①泰…　②郑…　Ⅲ.①英语－汉语－对照读物　②诗集－印度－现代　Ⅳ.①H319.4: I

中国版本图书馆CIP数据核字(2017)第108695号

**出版发行**/中译出版社
地　　址/北京市西城区车公庄大街甲4号物华大厦6层
电　　话/(010) 68359827；　68359303（发行部）；　53601537（编辑部）
邮　　编/100044
传　　真/(010) 68357870
电子邮箱/book@ctph.com.cn
网　　址/http://www.ctph.com.cn

总 策 划/张高里
策划编辑/胡晓凯
责任编辑/胡晓凯　范祥镇

封面设计/潘　峰
排　　版/北京竹页文化传媒有限公司
印　　刷/保定市中画美凯印刷有限公司
经　　销/新华书店

规　　格/710毫米×1000毫米　1/16
印　　张/8.25
字　　数/122千字
版　　次/2017年6月第一版
印　　次/2018年4月第二次

ISBN 978-7-5001-5278-1　定价：18.00元

中 译 出 版 社

多年以来，中译出版社有限公司（原中国对外翻译出版有限公司）凭借国内一流的翻译和出版实力及资源，精心策划、出版了大批双语读物，在海内外读者中和业界内产生了良好、深远的影响，形成了自己鲜明的出版特色。

二十世纪八九十年代出版的英汉（汉英）对照"一百丛书"，声名远扬，成为一套最权威、最有特色且又实用的双语读物，影响了一代又一代英语学习者和中华传统文化研究者、爱好者；还有"英若诚名剧译丛""中华传统文化精粹丛书""美丽英文书系"，这些优秀的双语读物，有的畅销，有的常销不衰反复再版，有的被选为大学英语阅读教材，受到广大读者的喜爱，获得了良好的社会效益和经济效益。

"双语名著无障碍阅读丛书"是中译专门为中学生和英语学习者精心打造的又一品牌，是一个新的双语读物系列，具有以下特点：

选题创新——该系列图书是国内第一套为中小学生量身打造的双语名著读物，所选篇目均为教育部颁布的语文新课标必读书目，或为中学生以及同等文化水平的社会读者喜闻乐见的世界名著,重新编译为英汉(汉英)对照的双语读本。这些书既给青少年读者提供了成长过程中不可或缺的精神食粮,又让他们领略到原著的精髓和魅力,对他们更好地学习英文大有裨益;同时,丛书中入选的《论语》《茶馆》《家》等汉英对照读物,亦是热爱中国传统文化的中外读者所共知的经典名篇,能使读者充分享受阅读经典的无限乐趣。

无障碍阅读——中学生阅读世界文学名著的原著会遇到很多生词和文化难点。针对这一情况,我们给每一本读物原文中的较难词汇和不易理解之处都加上了注释,在内文的版式设计上也采取英汉(或汉英)对照方式,扫清了学生阅读时的障碍。

优良品质——中译双语读物多年来在读者中享有良好口碑,这得益于作者和出版者对于图书质量的不懈追求。"双语名著无障碍阅读丛书"继承了中译双语读物的优良传统——精选的篇目、优秀的译文、方便实用的注解,秉承着对每一个读者负责的精神,竭力打造精品图书。

愿这套丛书成为广大读者的良师益友,愿读者在英语学习和传统文化学习两方面都取得新的突破。

# 目录 CONTENTS

The Home

家庭 ·································· 003

On the Seashore

海边 ·································· 005

The Source

来源 ·································· 007

Babys Way

孩童之道 ·························· 009

The Unheeded Pageant

不被注意的花饰 ················ 013

Sleep-Stealer

偷睡眠者 ·························· 017

The Beginning

开始 ·································· 021

Babys World

孩童的世界 ······················ 025

# 目
CONTENTS
# 录

When and Why

时候与原因 ·················································· 027

Defamation

责备 ··························································· 029

The Judge

审判官 ························································ 031

Playthings

玩具 ··························································· 033

The Astronomer

天文家 ························································ 035

Clouds and Waves

云与波 ························································ 037

The Champa Flower

金色花 ························································ 041

Fairyland

仙人世界 ····················································· 045

# 目
## CONTENTS
# 录

The Land of the Exile

流放的地方 ·················· 049

The Rainy Day

雨天 ·················· 053

Paper Boats

纸船 ·················· 057

The Sailor

水手 ·················· 059

The Further Bank

对岸 ·················· 063

The Flower-School

花的学校 ·················· 067

The Merchant

商人 ·················· 069

Sympathy

同情 ·················· 073

# 目
## 录
CONTENTS

Vocation

职业 ···················································· 075

Superior

长者 ···················································· 079

The Little Big Man

小大人 ················································· 081

Twelve O'clock

十二点钟 ·············································· 085

Authorship

著作家 ················································· 087

The Wicked  Postman

恶邮差 ················································· 091

The Hero

英雄 ···················································· 095

The End

告别 ···················································· 101

# 目
CONTENTS

The Recall

追唤 ···································· 105

The First Jasmines

第一次的茉莉 ······················ 107

The Banyan Tree

榕树 ···································· 109

Benediction

祝福 ···································· 111

The Gift

赠品 ···································· 113

My Song

我的歌 ································ 115

The Child-Angel

孩提之天使 ·························· 117

The Last Bargain

最后的契约 ·························· 119

*Rabindranath Tagore*

# The Home

I paced alone on the road across the field while the sunset was hiding its last gold like a **miser**①.

The daylight sank deeper and deeper into the darkness, and the **widowed**② land, whose harvest had been **reaped**③, lay silent.

Suddenly a boy's **shrill**④ voice rose into the sky. He **traversed**⑤ the dark unseen, leaving the track of his song across the **hush**⑥ of the evening.

His village home lay there at the end of the waste land, beyond the **sugar-cane**⑦ field, hidden among the shadows of the banana and the slender **areca palm**⑧, the **cocoa-nut**⑨ and the dark green **jack-fruit**⑩ tress.

I stopped for a moment in my lonely way under the starlight, and saw spread before me the darkened earth surrounding with her arms countless homes furnished with **cradles**⑪ and beds, mothers' hearts and evening lamps, and young lives glad with a gladness that knows nothing of its value for the world.

# 家庭

① miser ['maizə] *n.* 守财
奴；财迷
② widowed ['widəud] *v.*
（widow 的过去分词）
［罕用语］从……夺走
③ reap [ri:p] *v.* 收割，从
（地里）收割庄稼
④ shrill [ʃril] *a.* 尖声的
⑤ traverse ['trævəs] *v.* 越
过，穿过
⑥ hush [hʌʃ] *n.* 安静，寂
静
⑦ sugar-cane ['ʃugə,kein]
*n.*【植物】甘蔗
⑧ areca palm【植物】槟榔
（树）
⑨ cocoa-nut ['kəukə,nʌt] *n.*
（=coconut）椰子
⑩ jack-fruit ['dʒækfru:t] *n.*
【植物】木菠萝
⑪ cradle ['kreidl] *n.* 摇篮

我独自在横跨过田地的路上走着，夕阳像一个守财
奴似的，正藏起它的最后的金子。

白昼更加深沉地投入黑暗之中，那已经收割了的孤
寂的田地，默默地躺在那里。

天空里突然升起了一个男孩子的尖锐的歌声，他穿
过看不见的黑暗，留下他的歌声的辙痕跨过黄昏的静谧。

他的乡村的家坐落在荒凉的土地的边上，在甘蔗田
的后面，躲藏在香蕉树，瘦长的槟榔树，椰子树和深绿
色的贾克果树的阴影里。

我在星光下独自走着的路上停留了一会，我看见黑
沉沉的大地展开在我的面前，用她的手臂拥抱着无量数
的家庭，在那些家庭里，有着摇篮和床铺，母亲们的心
和夜晚的灯，还有年轻轻的生命，他们满心欢乐，却浑
然不知这样的欢乐对于世界的价值。

# On the Seashore

On the seashore of endless worlds children meet.

The infinite sky is motionless overhead and the restless water is **boisterous**①. On the seashore of endless worlds the children meet with shouts and dances.

They build their houses with sand, and they play with empty shells. With **withered**② leaves they weave their boats and smilingly float them on the vast deep. Children have their play on the seashore of worlds.

They know not how to swim, they know not how to **cast**③ nets. Pearl-fishers dive for pearls, merchants sail in their ships, while children gather pebbles and scatter them again. They seek not for hidden treasures, they know not how to cast nets.

The sea **surges up**④ with laughter, and pale gleams the smile of the sea-beach. Death-dealing waves sing meaningless **ballads**⑤ to the children, even like a mother while rocking her baby's cradle. The sea plays with children, and pale gleams the smile of the sea beach.

On the seashore of endless worlds children meet. **Tempest**⑥ roams in the **pathless**⑦ sky, ships are wrecked in the **trackless**⑧ water, death is abroad and children play. On the seashore of endless worlds is the great meeting of children.

# 海边

小孩子们会集在这无边际的世界的海边。

无限的天穹静止地临于头上，不息的海水在足下汹涌着。小孩子们会集在这无边无际的世界的海边，叫着跳着。

他们拿沙来建筑房屋，拿空贝壳来做游戏。他们把落叶编成了船，微笑地把他们放到广大的深海上。小孩子们在这世界的海边，做他们的游戏。

他们不知道怎样泅水，他们不知道怎样放网。采珠的人为了珠下水，商人在他们的船上航行，小孩子们却只把小圆石聚了又散。他们不搜求藏宝；他们不知道怎样放网。

海水带着笑掀起波浪，海边也淡淡地闪耀着微笑。致人死命的波涛，对着小孩子们唱无意义的歌曲，很像一个摇动她孩子的摇篮时的母亲，海水和小孩子们一同游戏，海边也淡淡地闪耀着微笑。

小孩子们会集在这无边无际的海边。狂风暴雨飘游在无辙迹的天空上，航船沉碎在无辙迹的海水里，死正在外面走着，小孩子们却在游戏。在这无边无际的世界的海边上，小孩子们大会集着。

① boisterous ['bɔistərəs] *a.*（大海）汹涌的

② withered ['wiðəd] *a.* 凋谢的

③ cast [kɑ:st] *v.* 撒（网）

④ surge up 浪涌，汹涌澎湃

⑤ ballad ['bæləd] *n.* 歌谣

⑥ tempest ['tempist] *n.* 暴风雨

⑦ pathless ['pɑ:θlis] *a.* 无人迹的

⑧ trackless ['træklis] *a.* 不留痕迹的

# The Source

The sleep that **flits**[1] on baby's eyes—does anybody know from where it comes? Yes, there is a rumour that it has its dwelling where, in the fairy village among shadows of the forest dimly lit with **glow-worms**[2], there hang two shy buds of **enchantment**[3]. From there it comes to kiss baby's eyes.

The smile that **flickers**[4] on baby's lips when he sleeps  does anybody know where it was born? Yes, there is a rumour that a young pale beam of a **crescent moon**[5] touched the edge of a vanishing autumn cloud, and there the smile was first born in the dream of a dew-washed morning—the smile that flickers on baby's lips when he sleeps.

The sweet, soft freshness that blooms on baby's limbs—does anybody know where it was hidden so long? Yes, when the mother was a young girl it lay **pervading**[6] her heart in tender and silent mystery of love—the sweet, soft freshness that has bloomed on baby's limbs.

# 来源

① flit [flit] *v.* 轻快地过去，掠过

② glow-worm ['gləuwə:m] *n.*【昆虫】萤火虫

③ enchantment [in'tʃɑ:ntmənt] *n.* 迷人的东西

④ flicker ['flikə] *v.* 闪动

⑤ crescent moon 新月

⑥ pervade [pə:'veid] *v.* 充满

　　流泛在孩子两眼的睡眠，——有谁知道他是从什么地方来的？是的，有个谣传，说他是住在萤火虫朦胧地照着的林影里的仙村里，在那个地方挂着两个迷人的惧怯的蓓蕾。他便是从那个地方来吻着孩子的两眼的。

　　当孩子睡时，微笑在他唇上浮动着，——有谁知道他是从什么地方生出来的？是的，有个谣传，说，一线新月的幼嫩的清光，触着将消未消的秋云边上，微笑便在那个地方初生在一个浴在清露里的早晨的梦中了。

　　甜蜜柔嫩的新鲜情景，在孩子的四肢上展放着，——有谁知道他在什么地方藏得这样久？是的，当母亲是一个少女的时候，他已在爱的温柔而沉静的神秘中，潜伏在她的心里。——甜蜜柔嫩的新鲜情景，在孩子的四肢上展放着。

# Babys Way

If baby only wanted to, he could fly up to heaven this moment.

It is not for nothing that he does not leave us.

He loves to rest his head on mother's bosom, and cannot ever bear to lose sight of her.


Baby knows all **manner**① of wise words, though few on earth can understand their meaning.

It is not for nothing that he never wants to speak.

The one thing he wants is to learn mother's words from mother's lips. That is why he looks so innocent.


Baby had a **heap**② of gold and pearls, yet he came like a beggar on to this earth.

It is not for nothing he came in such a **disguise**③.

This dear little naked **mendicant**④ pretends to be utterly helpless, so that he may beg for mother's wealth of love.


Baby was so free from every tie in the land of the tiny crescent moon.

# 孩童之道

只要孩童是愿意，他此刻便可飞上天去。

他所以不离开我们，并不是没有原故[1]。

他爱把他的头倚在母亲的胸间，就是一刻不见她，也是不行的。

孩童知道所有各种的聪明话，虽然这些话世间的人很少懂得它们的意义。

他所以永不想说，并不是没有原故。

他所要的一件事，就是要去学从母亲的唇里说出来的话。那就是他所以看来这样天真的原故了。

孩童有了一堆黄金与珠子，但他到这个世界上来，却像一个乞丐。

他所以这样假装了来，并不是没有原故。

这个可爱的小小的裸着身体的乞丐所以假装着完全无助的样子，便是想要乞求母亲的爱的资产。

孩童在纤小的新月的世界里，是一切束缚都没有的。

① manner ['mænə] *n.* 类型，种类

② heap [hi:p] *n.* (一) 堆

③ disguise [dis'gaiz] *n.* 假装

④ mendicant ['mendikənt] *n.* 乞丐

---

1 现在规范词形写作"缘故"。

It was not for nothing he gave up his freedom.

He knows that there is room for endless joy in mother's little corner of a heart, and it is sweeter far than liberty to be caught and pressed in her dear arms.

Baby never knew how to cry. He dwelt in the land of perfect **bliss**①.

It is not for nothing he has chosen to shed tears.

Though with the smile of his dear face he draws mother's **yearning**② heart to him, yet his little cries over tiny troubles weave the double bond of pity and love.

他所以弃了他的自由，并不是没有原故。

他知道有无穷的快乐藏在母亲的心的小小一隅里，被母亲亲爱的手臂所捉所抱，其甜美远胜过自由。

① bliss [blis] *n.* 极乐

孩童永不知道如何啼哭。他所住的是完全的乐土。

他所以要流泪，并不是没有原故。

② yearning [jə:niŋ] *a.* 渴望的

虽然他用了可爱的脸儿上的微笑，引逗得他母亲的热望的心向着他，然而他的因为细故而啼的小哭声却编成了怜与爱的两股带子。

# The Unheeded① Pageant②

Ah, who was it coloured that little **frock**③, my child, and covered your sweet limbs with that little red **tunic**④?

You have come out in the morning to play in the courtyard, **tottering**⑤ and **tumbling**⑥ as you run.

But who was it coloured that little frock, my child?

What is it makes you laugh, my little life-bud?

Mother smiles at you standing on the **threshold**⑦.

She claps her hands and her bracelets jingle, and you dance with your bamboo stick in your hand like a tiny little shepherd.

But what is it makes you laugh, my little life-bud?

O beggar, what do you beg for, clinging to your mother's neck with both your hands?

O greedy heart, shall I **pluck**⑧ the world like a fruit from the sky to place it on your little rosy palm?

O beggar, what are you begging for?

The wind carries away in **glee**⑨ the tinkling of your **anklet**⑩ bells.

# 不被注意的花饰

① unheeded [ˌʌnˈhiːdid] *a.* 未受到注意的
② pageant [ˈpædʒənt] *n.* 虚饰
③ frock [frɔk] *n.* 罩衫
④ tunic [ˈtjuːnik] *n.*（儿童等穿的长及臀部的宽大短外套式的）束腰外衣
⑤ totter [ˈtɔtə] *v.* 蹒跚而行
⑥ tumble [ˈtʌmbl] *v.* 跌跌撞撞地走
⑦ threshold [ˈθreʃhəuld] *n.* 门口

啊，谁给那件小外衫染上颜色的，我的孩子，谁使你的温软的肢体穿上那件红的小外衫的？

你在早晨就跑出来到天井里玩儿，你，跑着就像摇摇欲跌似的。

但是谁给那件小外衫染上颜色的，我的孩子？

什么事叫你大笑起来的，我的小小的命芽儿？

妈妈站在门边，微笑地望着你。

她拍着她的双手，她的手镯叮当地响着，你手里拿着你的竹竿儿在跳舞，活像一个小小的牧童。

但是什么事叫你大笑起来的，我的小小的命芽儿？

喔，乞丐，你双手攀搂住妈妈的头颈，要乞讨些什么？

喔，贪得无厌的心，要我把整个世界从天上摘下来，像摘一个果子似的，把它放在你的一双小小的玫瑰色的手掌上么？

喔，乞丐，你要乞讨些什么？

⑧ pluck [plʌk] *v.* 采，摘

⑨ glee [ˈgliː] *n.* 欢乐，高兴
⑩ anklet [ˈæŋklit] *n.* 脚镯

风高兴地带走了你踝铃的叮当。

The sun smiles and watches your **toilet**①.

The sky watches over you when you sleep in your mother's arms, and the morning comes tiptoe to your bed and kisses your eyes.

The wind carries away in glee the tinkling of your anklet bells.

The fairy mistress of dreams is coming towards you, flying through the **twilight**② sky.

The world-mother keeps her seat by you in your mother's heart.

He who plays his music to the stars is standing at your window with his flute.

And the fairy mistress of dreams is coming towards you, flying through the twilight sky.

① toilet ['tɔilit] *n.* 打扮

太阳微笑着，望着你的打扮。

当你睡在你妈妈的臂弯里时，天空在上面望着你，而早晨蹑手蹑脚地走到你的床跟前，吻着你的双眼。

风高兴地带走了你踝铃的叮当。

仙乡里的梦婆飞过朦胧的天空，向你飞来。

② twilight ['twailait] *a.* 模糊的，朦胧的

在你妈妈的心头上，那世界母亲，正和你坐在一块儿。

他，向星星奏乐的人，正拿着他的横笛，站在你的窗边。

仙乡里的梦婆飞过朦胧的天空，向你飞来。

# Sleep-Stealer[①]

Who stole sleep from baby's eyes? I must know.

**Clasping**[②] her **pitcher**[③] to her waist, mother went to fetch water from the village near by.

It was noon. The children's playtime was over; the ducks in the pond were silent.

The shepherd boy lay asleep under the shadow of the **banyan tree**[④].

The crane stood grave and still in the **swamp**[⑤] near the mango **grove**[⑥].

In the meanwhile the Sleep-stealer came and, **snatching**[⑦] sleep from baby's eyes, flew away.

When mother came back she found baby travelling the room over **on all fours**[⑧].

Who stole sleep from our baby's eyes? I must know. I must find her and chain her up.

I must look into that dark cave, where, through **boulders**[⑨] and **scowling**[⑩] stones, trickles a tiny stream.

I must search in the **drowsy**[⑪] shade of the *bakula*[⑫] grove, where pigeons coo in their corner, and fairies' anklets tinkle in the stillness of starry nights.

In the evening I will peep into the whispering silence of the bamboo forest,

# 偷睡眠者

① stealer ['sti:lə] *n.* 小偷
② clasp [klɑːsp] *v.* 紧紧抓
住
③ pitcher ['pitʃə] *n.*（有嘴
和柄的）大水罐

④ banyan tree【植物】印
度榕树
⑤ swamp [swɔmp] *n.* 沼泽
⑥ grove [grəuv] *n.* 果树林
⑦ snatch [snætʃ] *v.* 突然抓
取，夺

⑧ on all fours 匍匐着，爬
着

⑨ boulder ['bəuldə] *n.* 圆石
⑩ scowling [skauliŋ] *v.*
（scowl 的现在分词）皱
眉头
⑪ drowsy ['drauzi] *a.* 沉寂
的
⑫ bakula〈印〉醉花

谁从孩子的眼里把睡眠偷了去呢？我一定要知道。

母亲把她的水罐捧在腰间，走到近村汲水去了。

这是正午的时候。孩子们游戏的时间已经过去了；
池中的鸭子沉默无声。

牧童躺在榕树的荫下睡着了。

白鹤庄重而静定地立在檬果树[1]边的泥泽里。

就在这个时候，偷睡眠者便来了，她从孩子的两眼
里捉住睡眠，便飞去了。

当母亲回来时，她看见孩子四肢着地地在屋里爬
着。

谁从孩子的眼里把睡眠偷了去呢？我一定要知道。
我定要找到她，把她锁起来。

我定要向那个黑洞里张望着，在这个洞里，有一道
小泉从圆的和有皱纹的石上滴下来。

我定要在嘟句蓝[2]林中的阴沉沉的树影搜寻去，在
这个林里，鸽子在它们住的地方咕咕地叫着，仙女的脚

---

1 即芒果树。
2 "嘟句蓝花"（Bakula）译义作"醉花"，学名 mimusopselengi。
印度传说美女口中吐出香液，此花始开。

where fire-flies **squander**① their light, and will ask every creature I meet, "Can anybody tell me where the Sleep-stealer lives?"

Who stole sleep from baby's eyes? I must know.

Shouldn't I give her a good lesson if I could only catch her!

I would **raid**② her nest and see where she **hoards**③ all her stolen sleep.

I would **plunder**④ it all, and carry it home.

I would bind her two wings **securely**⑤, set her on the bank of the river, and then let her play at fishing with a reed among the **rushes**⑥ and **water-lilies**⑦.

When the marketing is over in the evening, and the village children sit in their mothers' laps, then the night birds will **mockingly**⑧ **din**⑨ her ears with:

"Whose sleep will you steal now?"

① squander ['skwɔndə] v.
挥霍，浪费

② raid [reid] v. 突然袭击

③ hoard [hɔːd] v. 贮藏

④ plunder ['plʌndə] v. 掠
夺，劫掠

⑤ securely [si'kjuəli] ad. 牢
固地

⑥ rush [rʌʃ] n.【植物】灯
芯草

⑦ water-lily ['wɔːtə,lili] n.
【植物】睡莲

⑧ mockingly ['mɔkiŋli] ad.
嘲笑地

⑨ din [din] v. 絮聒不休地
说

环在繁星满天的静夜里叮当地响着。

　　我要在黄昏时，向竹林的萧萧的静景里窥望着，在这林中，萤火虫闪闪地耗费它们的光明，只要遇见一个人，我便要问道："谁能告诉我偷睡眠者住在什么地方呢？"

　　谁从孩子的眼里把睡眠偷了去呢？我一定要知道。

　　只要我能捉住她，怕不会给她一顿好教训！

　　我要闯入她的巢穴，看她把所有偷来的睡眠藏在什么地方。

　　我要把它都夺了来，带回家去。

　　我要把她的双翼缚得紧紧的，把她放在河岸，然后叫她拿一根芦草，在灯芯草和睡莲间钓鱼为戏。

　　当黄昏时，街上已经收了市，村里的孩子们都坐在她母亲的膝上，于是那些夜鸟便讥笑地在她耳边说道：

　　"你现在还想偷谁的睡眠呢？"

# The Beginning

"Where have I come from, where did you pick me up?" the baby asked its mother.

She answered half crying, half laughing, and clasping the baby to her breast,—

"You were hidden in my heart as its desire, my darling.

You were in the dolls of my childhood's games; and when with clay I made the image of my god every morning, I made and unmade you then.

You were **enshrined**[1] with our household **deity**[2], in his worship I worshipped you.

In all my hopes and my loves, in my life, in the life of my mother you have lived.

In the lap of the deathless Spirit who rules our home you have been nursed **for ages**[3].

When in girlhood my heart was opening its petals, you **hovered**[4] as a fragrance about it.

Your tender softness bloomed in my youthful limbs, like a glow in the sky before the sunrise.

Heaven's first darling, twin-born with the morning light, you have floated

# 开始

"我是从哪儿来的，你，在哪儿把我捡起来的？"孩子问他的妈妈说。

她把孩子紧紧地搂在胸前，半哭半笑地答道——

"你曾被我当作心愿藏在我的心里，我的宝贝。

"你曾存在于我孩童时代玩的泥娃娃身上；每天早晨我用泥土塑造我的神像，那时我反复地塑了又捏碎了的就是你。

"你曾和我们的家庭守护神一同受到祀奉，我崇拜家神时也就崇拜了你。

"你曾活在我所有的希望和爱情里，活在我的生命里，我母亲的生命里。

"在主宰着我们家庭的不死的精灵的膝上，你已经被抚育了好多代了。

"当我做女孩子的时候，我的心的花瓣儿张开，你就像一股花香似地散发出来。

"你的软软的温柔，在我的青春的肢体上开花了，像太阳出来之前的天空上的一片曙光。

"上天的第一宠儿，晨曦的孪生兄弟，你从世界的

① enshrine [in'ʃrain] v. 奉祀
② deity ['di:iti] n. 神

③ for ages 很久

④ hover ['hɔvə] v. 升腾

down the stream of the world's life, and at last you have **stranded**① on my heart.

As I gaze on your face, mystery **over-whelms**② me; you who belong to all have become mine.

For fear of losing you I hold you tight to my breast. What magic has **snared**③ the world's treasure in these slender arms of mine?"

① strand [strænd] *v.* 搁浅
② over-whelm [ˌəuvəˈhwelm]
　　*v.* 淹没


③ snare [snɛə] *v.* 诱使

生命的溪流浮泛而下，终于停泊在我的心头。

　　"当我凝视你的脸蛋儿的时候，神秘之感淹没了我；你这属于一切人的，竟成了我的。

　　"为了怕失掉你，我把你紧紧地搂在胸前。是什么魔术把这世界的宝贝引到我这双纤小的手臂里来呢？"

# Babys World

I wish I could take a quiet corner in the heart of my baby's very own world.

I know it has stars that talk to him, and a sky that **stoops**① down to his face to amuse him with its silly clouds and rainbows.

Those who **make believe**② to be dumb, and look as if they never could move, come creeping to his window with their stories and with **trays**③ crowded with bright toys.

I wish I could travel by the road that crosses baby's mind, and out beyond all bounds;

Where messengers **run errands**④ for no cause between the kingdoms of kings of no history;

Where Reason makes kites of her laws and flies them, and Truth sets Fact free from its **fetters**⑤.

# 孩童的世界

① stoop [stu:p] *v.* 俯身

② make believe 假装
③ tray [trei] *n.* 托盘

④ run errands 办差事，跑腿

⑤ fetter ['fetə] *n.* 〔通常用复数〕桎梏

我愿我能在我孩童的世界之心里，占一角清净地。

我知道有群星同他说话，天空也在他面前垂下，用蒙蒙的云和彩虹来娱悦他。

那些大家以为他是哑的人，那些看去像是永不会走动的人，都来，都带了他们的故事，捧了满装着玩具的盘子，匍匐地来到他的窗前。

我愿我能在横过孩童心中的道路上游行，超越了一切的束缚；

在那儿，使者奉了无所谓的使命奔走于无史的诸王的王国间；

在那儿，理智以她的法律造为纸鸢而飞放，真理也使事实从桎梏中自由了。

# When and Why

When I bring you coloured toys, my child, I understand why there is such a play of colours on clouds, on water, and why flowers are painted in **tints**① —when I give coloured toys to you, my child.

When I sing to make you dance, I truly know why there is music in leaves, and why waves send their **chorus**② of voices to the heart of the listening earth—when I sing to make you dance.

When I bring sweet things to your greedy hands, I know why there is honey in the cup of the flower, and why fruits are secretly filled with sweet juice—when I bring sweet things to your greedy hands.

When I kiss your face to make you smile, my darling, I surely understand what pleasure streams from the sky in morning light, and what delight the summer **breeze**③ brings to my body—when I kiss you to make you smile.

# 时候与原因

① tint [tint] *n.* 色彩

当我给你五颜六色的玩具的时候，我的孩子，我明白了为什么云上水上是这样的色彩缤纷，为什么花朵上染上绚烂的颜色的原因了——当我给你五颜六色的玩具的时候，我的孩子。

② chorus ['kɔ:rəs] *n.* 合唱

当我唱着使你跳舞的时候，我真的知道了为什么树叶儿响着音乐，为什么波浪把它们的合唱的声音送进静听着的大地的心头的原因了——当我唱着使你跳舞的时候。

当我把糖果送到你贪得无厌的双手上的时候，我知道了为什么在花萼里会有蜜，为什么水果里会秘密地充溢了甜汁的原因了——当我把糖果送到你贪得无厌的双手上的时候。

③ breeze [bri:z] *n.* 风，尤指微风

当我吻着你的脸蛋儿叫你微笑的时候，我的宝贝，我的确明白了在晨光里从天上流下来的是什么样的快乐，而夏天的微风吹拂在我身体上的又是什么样的爽快——当我吻着你的脸蛋儿叫你微笑的时候。

# Defamation①

Why are those tears in your eyes, my child?

How **horrid**② of them to be always **scolding** you **for**③ nothing!

You have stained your fingers and face with ink while writing — is that why they call you dirty?

O, **fie**④! Would they dare to call the full moon dirty because it has **smudged**⑤ its face with ink?

For every little trifle they blame you, my child. They are ready to find fault for nothing.

You tore your clothes while playing — is that why they call you untidy?

O, fie! What would they call an autumn morning that smiles through its **ragged**⑥ clouds?

**Take no heed of**⑦ what they say to you, my child.

They make a long list of your **misdeeds**⑧.

Everybody knows how you love sweet things — is that why they call you greedy?

O, fie! What then would they call us who love you?

# 责备

为什么你眼里有了眼泪，我的孩子？

他们真是可怕，常常无谓地责备你。

你写字时墨污了你的手和脸——这就是他们所以骂你不洁的原故么？

呵，不对呀！他们也敢因为圆圆的月用墨涂了脸，便骂她为不洁么？

他们总要为了一件小事去责备你，我的孩子。他们总是无谓地寻人错处。

你游戏时扯破了你的衣裳——这就是他们所以说你不守规矩的原故么？

呵，不对呀！秋之晨从他的破碎的云衣中露出微笑，那么，他们要叫他什么呢？

他们对你说什么话，尽管可以不理他，我的孩子。

他们正把你做错的事列成一个长表。

谁都知道你是十分喜欢甜的东西的——这就是他们所以称你做贪婪的原故么？

呵！不对呀！我们是喜欢你的，那么，他们要叫我们什么呢？

# The Judge

Say of him what you please, but I know my child's **failings**①.

I do not love him because he is good, but because he is my little child.

How should you know how dear he can be when you try to **weigh** his merits **against**② his faults?

When I must punish him he becomes all the more a part of my being.

When I cause his tears to come my heart weeps with him.

I alone have a right to blame and punish, for he only may **chastise**③ who loves.

# 审判官

① failing ['feiliŋ] *n.* 缺点，
过失

② weigh against 把……
同……相权衡

③ chastise [tʃæs'taiz] *v.* 惩
处

你想说他什么尽管说罢，但是我知道我孩子的错处。

我爱他并不因为他好，只是因为他是我的孩子。

你如果把他的好处与坏处两两相权一下。恐怕你就会知道他是如何的可爱罢？

当我必须责罚他的时候，他更要成了我身的一部分了。

当我使他眼泪流出时，我的心也和他同哭了。

只有我才有权去骂他，去责罚他，因为只有爱人的才能惩戒人。

# Playthings<sup>①</sup>

Child, how happy you are sitting in the dust, playing with a broken **twig**② all the morning.

I smile at your play with that little bit of a broken twig.

I am busy with my accounts, adding up figures by the hour.

Perhaps you glance at me and think, "What a stupid game to spoil your morning with!"

Child, I have forgotten the art of being absorbed in sticks and **mud-pies**③.

I **seek out**④ costly playthings, and gather lumps of gold and silver.

With whatever you find you create your glad games, I spent both my time and my strength over things I never can obtain.

In my **frail**⑤ canoe I struggle to cross the sea of desire, and forget that I too am playing a game.

# 玩具

① plaything ['pleiθiŋ] *n.* 玩
具
② twig [twig] *n.* 细枝

③ mud-pie [,mʌd'pai] *n.*
（儿童玩的）泥团
④ seek out 找出

⑤ frail [freil] *a.* 易碎的，
脆弱的

孩子，你真是快活呀，一早晨坐在泥土里，耍着折
下来的小树枝儿。

我微笑地看你在那里耍着小枝的碎梗。

我正忙着算账，一小时一小时在那里加叠数字。

也许你在看我，想道："这种好没趣的游戏，竟把
你的一早晨的好时间夺去了！"

孩子，我忘了聚精会神耍枝子与泥饼的方法了。

我找出贵重的玩具，收集起金块，银块。

你呢，无论找到什么便去做你的快乐的游戏，我呢，
却把了我的时间与力气都费在那些我永不能得到的东西
上。

我在我的脆薄的独木船里，奋勉地航过欲望之海，
竟忘了我也是在那里做游戏了。

# The Astronomer<sup>①</sup>

I only said, "When in the evening the round full moon gets **entangled**<sup>②</sup> among the branches of that ***Kadam***<sup>③</sup> tree, couldn't somebody catch it?"

But **dādā**<sup>④</sup> laughed at me and said, "Baby, you are the silliest child I have ever known. The moon is ever so far from us, how could anybody catch it?"

I said, "Dādā, how foolish you are! When mother looks out of her window and smiles down at us playing, would you call her far away?"

Still dādā said, "You are a stupid child! But, baby, where could you find a net big enough to catch the moon with?"

I said, "Surely you could catch it with your hands."

But dādā laughed and said, "You are the silliest child I have known. If it came nearer, you would see how big the moon is."

I said, "Dādā, what nonsense they teach at your school! When mother bends her face down to kiss us does her face look very big?"

But still dādā says, "You are a stupid child."

# 天文家

① astronomer [əˈstrɔnəmə]
*n.* 天文学家
② entangled [inˈtæŋgld] *v.*
（entangle 的过去分词）
缠住
③ Kadam〈印〉劫丹波
④ dādā〈印〉哥哥

　　我不过说："当傍晚圆圆的满月挂在劫丹波[1]的枝头时，有人能去捉它么？"

　　哥哥却对我笑道："孩子呀，你真是我第一次看见的傻孩子。月儿离我们这样远，谁能去捉他呢？"

　　我说："哥哥，你真傻！当母亲向窗外探望，微笑地往下看着我们游戏时，你也能说她远么？"

　　哥哥还只是说："你这傻孩子！但是，孩子，你到哪里去找大网，能捉得住这月儿的大网呢？"

　　我说："你自然可以用双手去捉住它呀。"

　　但是哥哥笑道："你真是我第一次才看见的傻孩子。如果月儿走近了，你便知道他是多大了。"

　　我说："哥哥，你们学校里所教的，真是没有意义！当母亲低下脸儿向我们亲嘴时，她的脸看来也是很大的么？"

　　但是哥哥还只是说："你真是一个傻孩子。"

---

1 "劫丹波"原名 Kadam，亦作 Kadamba，学名 Namlea Cadamba，茜草属植物，开大黄色花，木材亦作黄色，为观赏植物，亦译为"迦谈闻花"。

# Clouds and Waves

Mother, the folk who live up in the clouds **call out**① to me —

"We play from the time we wake till the day ends.

We play with the golden dawn, we play with the silver moon."

I ask, "But, how am I to get up to you?"

They answer, "Come to the edge of the earth, **lift up**② your hands to the sky, and you will be taken up into the clouds."

"My mother is waiting for me at home," I say. "How can I leave her and come?"

Then they smile and float away.

But I know a nicer game than that, mother.

I shall be the cloud and you the moon.

I shall cover you with both my hands, and our house-top will be the blue sky.

The folk who live in the waves call out to me —

"We sing from morning till night; on and on we travel and know not where we pass."

I ask, "But, how am I to join you?"

They tell me, "Come to the edge of the shore and stand with your eyes tight shut, and you will be carried out upon the waves."

# 云与波

① call out 大声叫喊

② lift up 举起

母亲，住在云端的人对我唤道——

"我们从醒的时候游戏到白日终止。

"我们与黄金色的曙光游戏，我们与银白色的月亮游戏。"

我问道："但是，我怎么能够上你那里去呢？"

他们答道："你到地球的边上来，举手向天，就可以被举于云端了。"

"我母亲在家里等我呢，"我说，"我怎么能离开她而来呢？"

于是他们微笑浮游而去。

但是我知道一件比这个更好的游戏，母亲。

我做云，你做月亮。

我用两只手遮盖你，我们的屋顶就是青碧的天空。

住在波上的人对我唤道——

"我们从早晨唱歌到晚上；我们前进前进地旅行，也不知我们所经过的是什么地方。"

我问道："但是我怎么能加入呢？"

他们告诉我说："来到岸旁，站在那里紧闭你的两眼，你就被带到波上来了。"

I say, "My mother always wants me at home in the evening—how can I leave her and go?"

Then they smile, dance and pass by.

But I know a better game than that.

I will be the waves and you will be a strange shore.

I shall roll on and on and on, and break upon your lap with laughter.

And no one in the world will know where we both are.

我说："我母亲傍晚的时候，常要我在家里——我怎么能离开她而去呢？"

于是他们微笑，跳舞地滚过去。

但是我知道一件比这个更好的游戏。

我是波，你是奇异的岸。

我要流滚而进，进，进，带着笑，碎在你的膝上。

没有一个人在世界上知道我们俩在什么地方。

# The Champa[1] Flower

Supposing I became a *champa* flower, just for fun, and grew on a branch high up that tree, and shook in the wind with laughter and danced upon the newly **budded**[2] leaves, would you know me, mother?

You would call, "Baby, where are you?" and I should laugh to myself and keep quite quiet.

I should **slyly**[3] open my petals and watch you at your work.

When after your bath, with wet hair spread on your shoulders, you walked through the shadow of the *champa* tree to the little court where you say your **prayers**[4], you would notice the scent of the flower, but not know that it came from me.

When after the midday meal you sat at the window reading *Ramayana*[5], and the tree's shadow fell over your hair and your lap, I should **fling**[6] my **wee**[7]

# 金色花

① champa〈印〉金色花

② bud [bʌd] v.（植物）发芽，萌芽，长出芽

③ slyly [ˈslaili] ad. 暗中，偷偷摸摸地

④ prayer [preə] n. 祷告，祈祷

⑤ Ramayana〈印〉《罗摩衍那》

⑥ fling [fliŋ] v. 挥动，投掷

⑦ wee [wi:] a. 很小的，微小的

设如我变了一朵"金色花"[1]。只为了好玩，生在那树的高枝上，笑着在风中摇摆，又在新生的树叶上跳舞，母亲，你会认识我么？

你要是叫道："孩子，你在哪里呀？"我暗地在那里匿笑，却一声儿不响。

我要静悄悄地开了花瓣儿，看着你做工。

当你沐浴后，湿发披在两肩，穿过"金色花"的林荫，走到你做祷告的小庭院时，你会嗅到这花的香气，却不知道这香气是从我身上来的。

当你吃过中饭，坐在窗前读《罗摩衍那》[2]，树荫落在你的发与膝上时，我便要投我的小小的影子在你书

---

1 "金色花"原名 Champa，亦作 Champak，学名 Michelia Champaca，印度圣树，木兰花属植物，开金黄色碎花。译名亦作"瞻波伽"，或"占博迦"。

2 《罗摩衍那》（Ramayana）为印度叙事诗，相传系第五世纪 Valmiki 作。全篇二万四千章，分为七卷，皆系叙述罗摩生平之作。罗摩即罗摩犍陀罗（Ramachandra），德萨罗札王（Dasaratha）之子，悉多（Sita）之夫。他于第二世（Treta Yaga）入世，为伟世奴神（Vishnu）第七化身。印人看他为英雄，有崇拜他如神的。

罗摩有三，都是传说上的人物：一即罗摩犍陀罗，二为婆罗萨罗摩（Parasa Rama），三为巴罗罗摩（Bala Rama）。普通说"罗摩"，都是指第一个。

little shadow on to the page of your book, just where you were reading.

But would you guess that it was the tiny shadow of your little child?

When in the evening you went to the **cowshed**① with the lighted lamp in your hand, I should suddenly drop on to the earth again and be your own baby once more, and beg you to tell me a story.

"Where have you been, you naughty child?"

"I won't tell you, mother." That's what you and I would say then.

上，正投在你所读的地方。

但是你会猜得出这就是你孩子的小影子么？

① cowshed ['kauʃed] *n.* 牛棚

当你黄昏时拿了灯到牛棚里去，我便要突然地再落到地上来，又成了你的孩子，求你讲故事给我听。

"你到哪里去了，你这坏孩子？"

"我不告诉你，母亲。"这就是你同我那时所要说的话了。

# Fairyland

If people came to know where my king's palace is, it would vanish into the air.

The walls are of white silver and the roof of shining gold.

The queen lives in a palace with seven courtyards, and she wears a jewel that cost all the wealth of seven kingdoms.

But, let me tell you, mother, in a whisper, where my king's palace is.

It is at the corner of our **terrace**① where the pot of the *tulsi*② plant stands.

The princess lies sleeping on the far-away shore of the seven impassable seas.

There is none in the world who can find her but myself.

She has bracelets on her arms and pearl **drops**③ in her ears; her hair sweeps down upon the floor.

She will wake when I touch her with my magic wand, and jewels will fall from her lips when she smiles.

But let me whisper in your ear, mother; she is there in the corner of our terrace where the pot of the *tulsi* plant stands.

# 仙人世界

如果人们知道了我的国王的宫殿在哪里．它就会消失在空气中的。

墙壁是白色的银，屋顶是耀眼的黄金。

皇后住在有七个庭院的宫苑里；她戴的一串珠宝，值得整整七个王国的全部财富。

不过，让我悄悄地告诉你，妈妈，我的国王的宫殿究竟在哪里。

它就在我们阳台的角上，在那栽着杜尔茜花的花盆放着的地方。

① terrace ['terəs] *n.*（房屋前面的）阳台
② tulsi〈印〉杜尔茜花

公主躺在远远的隔着七个不可逾越的重洋的那一岸沉睡着。

除了我自己，世界上便没有人能够找到她。

她臂上有镯子，她耳上挂着珍珠；她的头发拖到地板上。

当我用我的魔杖点触她的时候，她就会醒过来，而当她微笑时，珠玉将会从她唇边落下来。

不过，让我在你的耳朵边悄悄地告诉你，妈妈，她就住在我们阳台的角上，在那栽着杜尔茜花的花盆放着

③ drop [drɔp] *n.* 滴状物（如某些装饰物、球形耳坠）

When it is time for you to go to the river for your bath, step up to that terrace on the roof.

I sit on the corner where the shadows of the walls meet together.

Only **puss**[①] is allowed to come with me, for she knows where the barber in the story lives.

But let me whisper, mother, in your ear where the barber in the story lives.

It is at the corner of the terrace where the pot of the *tulsi* plant stands.

的地方。

当你要到河里洗澡的时候，你走上屋顶的那座阳台来罢。

我就坐在墙的阴影所聚会的一个角落里。

我只让小猫儿跟我在一起，因为它知道那故事里的理发匠住的地方。

不过，让我在你的耳朵边悄悄地告诉你，那故事里的理发匠到底住在哪里。

他住的地方，就在阳台的角上，在那栽着杜尔茜花的花盆放着的地方。

① puss [pus] *n.* ［爱称或儿语］（小）猫

# The Land Of the Exile①

Mother, the light has grown grey in the sky; I do not know what the time is.

There is no fun in my play, so I have come to you. It is Saturday, our holiday.

Leave off your work, mother; sit here by the window and tell me where the desert of **Tepāntar**② in the fairy tale is?

The shadow of the rains has covered the day from end to end.

The **fierce**③ lightning is **scratching**④ the sky with its nails.

When the clouds **rumble**⑤ and it thunders, I love to be afraid in my heart and **cling to**⑥ you.

When the heavy rain patters for hours on the bamboo leaves, and our windows shake and rattle at the **gusts**⑦ of wind, I like to sit alone in the room, mother, with you, and hear you talk about the desert of Tepāntar in the fairy tale.

Where is it, mother, on the shore of what sea, at the foot of what hills, in the kingdom of what king?

There are no **hedges**⑧ there to mark the fields, no footpath across it by which the villagers reach their village in the evening, or the woman who gathers

# 流放的地方

① exile ['egzail] *n.* 流放，放逐

妈妈，天空上的光成了灰色了；我不知道是什么时候了。

我玩得怪没劲儿的，所以到你这里来了。这是星期六，是我们的休息日。

② Tepāntar〈印〉特潘塔

放下你的活计，妈妈；坐在靠窗的一边，告诉我童话里的特潘塔沙漠在什么地方？

③ fierce [fiəs] *a.* 凶猛的，凶暴的
④ scratch [skrætʃ] *v.* 刮，擦
⑤ rumble ['rʌmbl] *v.* 隆隆作响
⑥ cling to 紧紧抓住
⑦ gust [gʌst] *n.*（风）一阵突发，突然一阵爆发

雨的影子遮掩了整个白天。

凶猛的电光用它的爪子抓着天空。

当乌云在轰轰地响着，天打着雷的时候，我总爱心里带着恐惧爬伏到你的身上。

当大雨倾泻在竹叶子上好几个钟头，而我们的窗户被狂风震得格格发响的时候，我就爱独自和你坐在屋里，妈妈，听你讲童话里的特潘塔沙漠的故事。

它在哪里，妈妈，在哪一个海洋的岸上，在哪些个山峰的脚下，在哪一个国王的国土里？

⑧ hedge [hedʒ] *n.* 界限

田地上没有此疆彼壤的界石，也没有村人在黄昏时走回家的，或妇人在树林里捡拾枯枝而捆载到市场上去

dry sticks in the forest can bring her load to the market. With **patches**① of yellow grass in the sand and only one tree where the pair of wise old birds have their nest, lies the desert of Tepāntar.

I can imagine how, on just such a cloudy day, the young son of the king is riding alone on a grey horse through the desert, in search of the princess who lies imprisoned in the giant's palace across that unknown water.

When the **haze**② of the rain comes down in the distant sky, and lightning starts up like **a** sudden **fit of**③ pain, does he remember his unhappy mother, abandoned by the king, sweeping the **cow-stall**④ and wiping her eyes, while he rides through the desert of Tepāntar in the fairy tale?

See, mother, it is almost dark before the day is over, and there are no travellers **yonder**⑤ on the village road.

The shepherd boy has gone home early from the **pasture**⑥, and men have left their fields to sit on **mats**⑦ under the **eaves**⑧ of their huts, watching the scowling clouds.

Mother, I have left all my books on the shelf—do not ask me to do my lessons now.

When I grow up and am big like my father, I shall learn all that must be learnt.

But just for to-day, tell me, mother, where the desert of Tepāntar in the fairy tale is?

① patch [pætʃ] *n.* 小块土地

② haze [heiz] *n.* 薄雾
③ a fit of 一阵
④ cow-stall [ˌkauˈstɔːl] *n.* 牛棚

⑤ yonder [jɔndə] *ad.* 在远处，那边
⑥ pasture [ˈpɑːstʃə] *n.* 牧场
⑦ mat [mæt] *n.* 草席
⑧ eaves [iːvz] *n.* [复] 屋檐

的道路。沙地上只有一小块一小块的黄色草地，只有一株树，就是那一对聪明的老鸟儿在那里做窝的，那个地方就是特潘塔沙漠。

我能够想象得到，就在这样一个乌云密布的日子，国王的年轻的儿子，怎样地独自骑着一匹灰色马，走过这个沙漠，去寻找那被囚禁在不可知的重洋之外的巨人宫里的公主。

当雨雾在遥远的天空下降，电光像一阵突然发作的痛楚的痉挛似地闪射的时候，他可记得他的不幸的母亲，为国王所弃，正在扫除牛棚，眼里流着眼泪，当他骑马走过童话里的特潘塔沙漠的时候？

看，妈妈，一天还没有完，天色就差不多黑了，那边村庄的路上没有什么旅客了。

牧童早就从牧场上回家了，人们都已从田地里回来，坐在他们草屋的檐下的草席上，眼望着阴沉的云块。

妈妈，我把我所有的书本都放在书架上了——不要叫我现在做功课。

当我长大了，大得像爸爸一样的时候，我将会学到必须学的东西的。

但是，今天你可得告诉我，妈妈，童话里的特潘塔沙漠在什么地方？

# The Rainy Day

**Sullen**① clouds are gathering fast over the black **fringe**② of the forest.

O child, do not go out!

The palm trees in a row by the lake are **smiting**③ their heads against the **dismal**④ sky; the crows with their **draggled**⑤ wings are silent on the **tamarind**⑥ branches, and the eastern bank of the river is **haunted**⑦ by a deepening gloom.

Our cow is **lowing**⑧ loud, tied at the fence.

O child, wait here till I bring her into the stall.

Men have crowded into the flooded field to catch the fishes as they escape from the over-flowing ponds; the rain water is running in **rills**⑨ through the narrow lanes like a laughing boy who has run away from his mother to tease her.

Listen, someone is shouting for the boatman at the **ford**⑩.

O child, the daylight is dim, and the crossing at the **ferry**⑪ is closed.

The sky seems to ride fast upon the madly-rushing rain; the water in the river is loud and impatient; women have **hastened**⑫ home early from the **Ganges**⑬ with their filled pitchers.

The evening lamps must be made ready.

# 雨天

① sullen ['sʌlən] *a.* 阴沉的
② fringe [frindʒ] *n.* 穗状物
③ smite [smait] *v.* 打；重击
④ dismal ['dizməl] *a.* 阴暗的
⑤ draggled ['drægld] *v.* （draggle 的过去分词）拖曳
⑥ tamarind ['tæmərind] *n.*【植物】罗望子树
⑦ haunt [hɔːnt] *v.* 缠住
⑧ low [ləu] *v.* （牛）哞哞叫
⑨ rill [ril] *n.* 小河，小溪

⑩ ford ['fɔːd] *n.* 浅滩
⑪ ferry ['feri] *n.* 渡口
⑫ hasten ['heisən] *v.* 赶快，赶紧
⑬ Ganges ['gændʒiːz] *n.* 恒河

雨云很快地集在森林的黑缨上面。

孩子，你不要出去呀！

湖边的一行棕树，用他们的头向暝暗的天空打着，敛着双翼的乌鸦们，静悄悄地栖在罗望子的枝上，河的东岸正为乌沉沉的暝色所侵袭。

我们的牛系在篱上，高声鸣着。

孩子，在这里等，等我先把牛牵进牛栏里去。

许多人都挤在池水泛滥的田间，捉那从泛滥的池中逃出来的鱼儿；雨水成了小河，流过狭弄，好像一个笑着的孩子从他母亲那里跑开，故意要恼她一样。

听呀，有人在浅滩上喊船夫呢。

孩子，天色暝暗了，渡头的摆渡已停了。

天空好像是在滂沱的雨上快跑着；河里的水喧叫而且暴躁；妇人们早已拿了汲满了水的水瓶，从恒河畔匆匆地回家。

夜里用的灯，要预备好了。

O child, do not go out!

The road to the market is **desolate**①, the lane to the river is slippery. The wind is roaring and struggling among the bamboo branches like a wild beast **tangled**② in a net.

孩子，不要出去呀！

到市场去的大道已没有人走，到河边去的小路又是很滑的。风在竹林里咆哮着，挣扎着，好像一只落在网中的野兽。

① desolate ['desələt] *a.* 荒无人烟的，荒凉的

② tangle ['tæŋgl] *v.* 缠结

# Paper Boats

Day by day I float my paper boats one by one down the running stream.

In big black letters I write my name on them and the name of the village where I live.

I hope that someone in some strange land will find them and know who I am.

I load my little boats with *shiuli*① flowers from our garden, and hope that these blooms of the dawn will be carried safely to land in the night.

I launch my paper boats and look up into the sky and see the little clouds setting their white **bulging**② sails.

I know not what playmate of mine in the sky sends them down the air to race with my boats!

When night comes I bury my face in my arms and dream that my paper boats float on and on under the midnight stars.

The fairies of sleep are sailing in them, and the **lading**③ is their baskets full of dreams.

# 纸船

我每天把纸船一个个放在急流的溪中。

我用大黑字写我的名字和我住的地名在纸船上。

我希望住在异地的人得到了这纸船，就知道我是谁。

我把园中长的希利花①载在这些小船上，希望这些黎明开的花能在夜里平平安安地带到岸上。

我投我的纸船到水里，仰看天空，看见小朵的云正张着满鼓②着风的白帆。

我不知道是不是天上的游伴把这些船放下来同我的船比赛！

夜来了，我的脸埋在手臂里，梦见我的纸船在中夜的星辰下面渐渐地浮泛上去。

"睡之仙人"坐在船里，带着他们满载③着梦的篮子。

① shiuli〈印〉希利花

② bulge [bʌldʒ] v. 鼓起来

③ lading ['leidiŋ] n.（装载的）货物

# The Sailor

The boat of the boatman Madhu is **moored**① at the **wharf**② of Rajgunj.

It is uselessly **laden with**③ **jute**④, and has been lying there **idle**⑤ for ever so long.

If he would only lend me his boat, I should **man**⑥ her with a hundred oars, and **hoist**⑦ sails, five or six or seven.

I should never **steer**⑧ her to stupid markets.

I should sail the seven seas and the thirteen rivers of fairyland.

But, mother, you won't weep for me in a corner.

I am not going into the forest like **Ramachandra**⑨ to come back only after fourteen years.

I shall become the prince of the story, and fill my boat with whatever I like.

I shall take my friend Ashu with me. We shall sail merrily across the seven seas and the thirteen rivers of fairyland.

# 水手

① moor [muə] v. 使停泊，
系泊
② wharf [hwɔ:f] n. 码头
③ laden with 装满的
④ jute [dʒu:t] n.【植物】黄
麻
⑤ idle ['aidl] a. 闲置的
⑥ man [mæn] v.【航海学】
为船的某部位配置水手
⑦ hoist [hɔist] v. 升起，拉
起
⑧ steer [stiə] v. 驾驶

⑨ Ramachandra〈印〉罗摩

　　船夫曼特胡的船只停泊在拉琪根琪码头。

　　这只船无用地装载着黄麻，无所事事地停泊在那里
已经好久了。

　　只要他肯把他的船借给我，我就给它安装一百只
桨，扬起五个或六个或七个布帆来。

　　我决不把它驾驶到愚蠢的市场上去。

　　我将航行遍仙人世界里的七个大海和十三条河道。


　　但是，妈妈，你不要躲在角落里为我哭泣。

　　我不会像罗摩犍陀罗[1]似的，到森林中去，一去
十四年才回来。

　　我将成为故事中的王子，把我的船装满了我所喜欢
的东西。

　　我将带我的朋友阿细和我做伴，我们要快快乐乐地
航行于仙人世界里的七个大海和十三条河道。

---

1　罗摩犍陀罗即罗摩。他是印度叙事诗《罗摩衍那》中的主角。为
了尊重父亲的诺言和维持弟兄间的友爱，他抛弃了继承王位的权利，
和妻子悉多在森林中被放逐了十四年。

We shall set sail in the early morning light.

When at **noontide**① you are bathing at the pond, we shall be in the land of a strange king.

We shall pass the ford of **Tirpurni**②, and leave behind us the desert of Tepāntar.

When we come back it will be getting dark, and I shall tell you of all that we have seen.

I shall cross the seven seas and the thirteen rivers of fairyland.

① noontide ['nu:ntaid] *n.* 中
午，正午

② Tripurni〈印〉特浦尼

我将在绝早的晨光里张帆航行。

中午，你正在池塘里洗澡的时候，我们将在一个陌
生的国王的国土上了。

我们将经过特浦尼浅滩，把特潘塔沙漠抛落在我们
的后边。

当我们回来的时候，天色快黑了，我将告诉你我们
所见到的一切。

我将越过仙人世界里的七个大海和十三条河道。

# The Further Bank

I long to go over there to the further bank of the river,

Where those boats are tied to the bamboo **poles**① in a line;

Where men cross over in their boats in the morning with **ploughs**② on their shoulders to **till**③ their far-away fields;

Where the cowherds make their lowing cattle swim across to the riverside pasture;

Whence they all come back home in the evening, leaving the **jackals**④ to **howl**⑤ in the island overgrown with weeds.

Mother, if you don't mind, I should like to become the boatman of the ferry when I am grown up.

They say there are strange pools hidden behind that high bank,

Where flocks of wild ducks come when the rains are over, and thick reeds grow round the margins where waterbirds lay their eggs;

Where **snipes**⑥ with their dancing tails **stamp**⑦ their tiny footprints upon the clean soft mud;

Where in the evening the tall grasses **crested**⑧ with white flowers invite the moonbeam to float upon their waves.

# 对岸

我想走过河的对岸去，

在那边，船只一行儿系在竹竿上；

人们在他们的船上，清早的渡过那边去，犁头置在肩上，去耕耘他们的远处的田：

在那边，牧人们使他们鸣叫着的牛游泳到河旁的牧场上去；

黄昏的时候，他们都回家了，只留着豺狼在这满长着野草的岛上哀叫。

母亲，如果你不在意，我长成的时候，要做这岸边的渡夫。

他们说有好些奇异的池塘藏在这个高岸之后。

雨过去了，一群一群的野鹜飞到那里去；茂厚的芦草在岸边四围生长，水鸟生他们的蛋在里面；

竹鸡们，带着他们的跳舞的尾巴印他们细小的足印在整齐的软泥上；

黄昏的时候，长草顶着白花邀月光在他们的波浪上浮游。

① pole [pəul] *n.* 杆
② plough [plau] *n.* 犁

③ till [til] *v.* 耕，犁

④ jackal ['dʒækɔ:l] *n.*【动物】豺，胡狼
⑤ howl [haul] *v.*（狼）嗥叫，长嚎

⑥ snipe [snaip] *n.*【鸟类】扇尾沙锥
⑦ stamp [stæmp] *v.* 踏，用力踩
⑧ crest [krest] *v.* 在……上加顶饰

Mother, if you don't mind, I should like to become the boatman of the ferryboat when I am grown up.

I shall cross and cross back from bank to bank, and all the boys and girls of the village will wonder at me while they are bathing.

When the sun climbs the mid sky and morning **wears on**① to noon, I shall come running to you, saying, "Mother, I am hungry!"

When the day is done and the shadows **cower**② under the trees, I shall come back in the dusk.

I shall never go away from you into the town to work like father.

Mother, if you don't mind, I should like to become the boatman of the ferryboat when I am grown up.

母亲，如果你不在意，我长成的时候要做这渡船里的渡夫。

① wear on（时间）慢慢地
流逝

② cower ['kauə] v. 蜷缩

我要自此岸至彼岸，渡过来，渡过去，所有村中男孩女孩，他们正在沐浴，都要奇怪我。

太阳升到中天，早晨变为正午了，我将跑到你那里去，说道："母亲，我饿了！"

日已完了，影子俯伏在树底下，我便要在黄昏中回家来。

我将永不同父亲一样，离开你到城里去做事，

母亲，如果你不在意，我长成的时候要做这渡船里的渡夫。

# The Flower-School

When storm clouds rumble in the sky and June showers come down,

The moist east wind comes marching over the **heath**① to blow its **bagpipes**②
among the bamboos.

Then crowds of flowers come out of a sudden, from nobody knows where,
and dance upon the grass in **wild**③ glee.

Mother, I really think the flowers go to school underground.

They do their lessons with doors shut, and if they want to come out to play
before it is time, their master makes them stand in a corner.

When the rains come they have their holidays.

Branches **clash**④ together in the forest, and the leaves rustle in the wild
wind, the thunder-clouds clap their giant hands and the flower children rush out
in dresses of pink and yellow and white.

Do you know, mother, their home is in the sky, where the stars are.

Haven't you seen how eager they are to get there? Don't you know why
they are in such a hurry?

Of course, I can guess to whom they raise their arms: they have their mother
as I have my own.

# 花的学校

① heath [hi:θ] *n.* 〈英〉（石南丛生的）荒地，荒野
② bagpipe ['bægpaip] *n.* ［常用复数，用作单数或复数］（苏格兰、爱尔兰等的）风笛
③ wild [waild] *a.* 极度兴奋的

④ clash [klæʃ] *v.* （大声）碰撞

当雷云在天上轰响着，六月的大雨落下的时候，润湿的东风走过荒野，在竹林中吹着口笛。

于是一群一群的花从无人知的地方突然走出来，在绿草上狂乐地跳着舞。

母亲，我实在以为群花是在地下上学的。

他们关了门上课，如果他们想在散学以前出外游戏，他们的先生是要罚他们站壁角的。

雨一来时，他们便放假了。

树枝在林中互相抵触着，绿叶在狂风里萧萧地响着，雷云拍着大手，花孩子们便在那时候穿了紫的，黄的，白的衣，急急地跑了出来。

你要知道，母亲，他们的家是在天上，在群星所住的地方。

你没有看见他们怎样想着要到那儿去么？你不知道他们为什么要那样匆忙么？

我自然能够猜得出他们是对谁扬起双臂来：他们也有母亲同我一样。

# The Merchant

Imagine, mother, that you are to stay at home and I am to travel into strange lands.

Imagine that my boat is ready at the landing fully laden.

Now think well, mother, before you say what I shall bring for you when I come back.

Mother, do you want heaps and heaps of gold?

There, by the banks of golden streams, fields are full of golden harvest.

And in the shade of the forest path the golden *champa* flowers drop on the ground.

I will gather them all for you in many hundred baskets.

Mother, do you want pearls big as the rain-drops of autumn?

I shall cross to the pearl island shore.

There in the early morning light pearls tremble on the **meadow**① flowers, pearls drop on the grass, and pearls are scattered on the sand in **spray**② by the **wild**③ sea-waves.

My brother shall have a pair of horses with wings to fly among the clouds.

# 商人

母亲，我们想象着，你住在家里，我到异邦去旅行。

再想象着，我的船已载了满船的东西，停在码头。

现在，母亲，先慢慢地想着，然后再告诉我，回来的时候要带些什么给你。

母亲，你要一堆一堆的黄金么？

在金河的两岸，田野里全是金色的稻实。

在林荫的路上，黄色花[1]也一朵一朵地落在地。

我要为你把它们全都收拾起来，放在好几百个篮子里。

母亲，你要像秋天的雨点一般大的珍珠么？

我要渡海到珍珠岛的岸上去。

那个地方，在清晨的曙光里，珠子都在草地的野花上颤动，珠子都落在绿草上，珠子都被汹狂的海浪撒在沙滩，成为水花。

我的哥哥呢，我要送他两只有翼的马，会在云端飞着的。

① meadow ['medəu] *n.* 草地
② spray [sprei] *n.* 水沫，浪花
③ wild [waild] *a.* 狂暴的

---

1　即前文所说的金色花，见第 41 页《金色花》。

For father I shall bring a magic pen that, without his knowing, will write of itself.

For you, mother, I must have the **casket**[1] and jewel that cost seven kings their kingdoms.

父亲呢，我要带一支有魔力的笔给他，那支笔不要父亲知道，它自己便会写出字来。

你呢，母亲，我一定要把那个值得七个王国的箱子和珠宝送给你。

① casket ['kɑ:skit] *n.* （贮藏珠宝的）小匣子

# Sympathy

If I were only a little puppy, not your baby, mother dear, would you say "No" to me if I tried to eat from your dish?

Would you **drive** me **off**①, saying to me, "Get away, you naughty little puppy?"

Then go, mother, go! I will never come to you when you call me, and never let you feed me any more.

If I were only a little green parrot, and not your baby, mother dear, would you keep me chained **lest**② I should fly away?

Would you shake your finger at me and say, "What an ungrateful **wretch**③ of a bird! It is **gnawing at**④ its chain day and night?"

Then, go, mother, go! I will run away into the woods; I will never let you take me in your arms again.

# 同情

如果我是一只小狗，而不是你的小孩，亲爱的母亲，当我想吃你的碟中之物时，你要向我说"不"么？

你要拉开我，对我说道，"滚开，你无用的小狗"么？

那么，走罢，母亲，走罢！当你叫唤我的时候，我要永不到你那里去，也永不要你再养活我了。

如果我是一只绿色的小鹦鹉，而不是你的小孩，亲爱的母亲，你要防守我的链子怕我飞走么？

你要对我摇你的手，说道，"怎么样一个不知感恩的贱鸟呀！整日整夜地只啮它的链子"么？

那么，走罢，母亲，走罢，我要跑到树林里去；我将永不再叫你抱我在你的臂里了。

① drive off 把……赶走

② lest [lest] conj. 以免，免得

③ wretch [retʃ] n. 坏家伙

④ gnaw at 咬，啃，啮

# Vocation

When the **gong**① sounds ten in the morning and I walk to school by our lane,

Everyday I meet the **hawker**② crying, "**Bangles**③, crystal bangles!"

There is nothing to hurry him on, there is no road he must take, no place he must go to, no time when he must come home.

I wish I were a hawker, spending my day in the road, crying, "Bangles, crystal bangles!"

When at four in the afternoon I come back from the school,

I can see through the gate of that house the gardener digging the ground.

He does what he likes with his spade, he **soils**④ his clothes with dust, nobody takes him to task if he gets baked in the sun or gets wet.

I wish I were a gardener digging away at the garden with nobody to stop me from digging.

Just as it gets dark in the evening and my mother sends me to bed,

I can see through my open window the **watchman**⑤ walking up and down.

The lane is dark and lonely and the street-lamp stands like a giant with one red eye in its head.

# 职业

早晨十点钟时，我沿着我们的街巷到学校里去，

每天在这个时候，我都遇见那个小贩，他叫道："镯子，透明的镯子！"

他不受事务的催促，他随意地走过这条街那条街，他没有一定的地方要去，他又没有一定的时间要回家。

我愿意我是一个小贩，在街上过日子，叫着："镯子，透明的镯子！"

下午四点钟时，我从学校里回家，

从一家门口，我看见一个园丁在那里掘地。

他用他的锄子，要怎么掘，便怎么掘，他被尘土污了衣裳，他或去晒太阳或是身上湿了，都没有人去骂他。

我愿意我是一个园丁，在花园里掘地，谁也不来阻止我。

天色刚黑时，母亲送我上床，

从开着的窗口，我能看见更夫在街上走来走去。

街上又黑又冷清，路灯立在那里，像一个头上生着一只红眼睛的巨人。

The watchman swings his lantern and walks with his shadow at his side, and never once goes to bed in his life.

I wish I were a watchman walking the streets all night, chasing the shadows with my lantern.

更夫摇着他的提灯，走来走去，他的影子也随在他身旁走着，他一生没有上床去过。

我愿意我是一个更夫，整夜在街上走，提了灯去追逐影子。

# Superior①

Mother, your baby is silly! She is so absurdly childish!

She does not know the difference between the lights in the streets and the stars.

When we **play at**② eating with pebbles, she thinks they are real food, and tries to put them into her mouth.

When I open a book before her and ask her to learn her a, b, c, she tears the leaves with her hands and roars for joy at nothing; this is your baby's way of doing her lesson.

When I shake my head at her in anger and scold her and call her naughty, she laughs and thinks it great fun.

Everybody knows that father is away, but, if in play I call aloud "Father," she looks about her in excitement and thinks that father is near.

When I hold my class with the donkeys that our **washerman**③ brings to carry away the clothes and I warn her that I am the school-master, she will scream for no reason and call me dādā.

Your baby wants to catch the moon. She is so funny; she calls Ganesh Gānush.

Mother, your baby is silly, she is so absurdly childish!

# 长者

① superior [sjuːˈpɪrɪə] *n.* 长者
② play at 做假装……的游戏

母亲，你的孩子是很傻的，她竟是这样的一个呆孩子！
她不知道街上的灯和天上的星的分别。

当我们游戏着，把小石当作食物时，她便以为它们真是吃的东西，竟想放进嘴里去。

当我翻开一本书，放在她面前，要她读 a，b，c，她却用手把书页撕了，无端快活地叫起来，这就是你的孩子读书的样子。

当我生气地对她摇头，骂着她，叫她玩皮 [1] 时，她却笑着，以为很有趣。

谁都知道父亲不在家，但如我高声戏叫一声"父亲"，她便要高兴地四面望着，以为父亲真是在近处。

③ washerman [ˈwɔʃəmən]
*n.* 男洗衣工

当我把洗衣人带来载衣服回去的驴子当作学生，我警告她说，我是先生，她却无故地叫起我哥哥来。

你的孩子要捉住月亮。她是这样的可笑；她把 Ganesh [2] 叫作 Gānush。

母亲，你的孩子是很傻的，她竟是这样的一个呆孩子！

---

1　现在规范词形写作"顽皮"。
2　Ganesh 是印度的一个普通名字，也是象头神之名。

# The Little Big Man

I am small because I am a little child. I shall be big when I am as old as my father is.

My teacher will come and say, "It is late, bring your **slate**① and your books."

I shall tell him, "Do you not know I am as big as father? And I must not have lessons any more."

My master will wonder and say, "He can leave his books if he likes, for he is grown up."

I shall dress myself and walk to the fair where the crowd is thick.

My uncle will come rushing up to me and say, "You will get lost, my boy; let me carry you."

I shall answer, "Can't you see, uncle, I am as big as father? I must go to the fair alone."

Uncle will say, "Yes, he can go wherever he likes, for he is grown up."

Mother will come from her bath when I am giving money to my nurse, for I shall know how to open the box with my key.

Mother will say, "What are you about, naughty child?"

I shall tell her, "Mother, don't you know, I am as big as father, and I must

# 小大人

我是细小的，因为我是一个小孩子。到了我像父亲一样老时，便要变大了。

我的先生要是走来说道："时候晚了，把你的石板，你的书拿来。"

我便要告诉你道："你不知道我已是同父亲一样大了么？我决不再学什么功课了。"

我的先生便将惊异地说道："他读书不读书可以随便，因为他是大人了。"

我将自己穿了衣裳，走到众人拥挤的市场里去。

我的叔父要是跑过来说："你要失路了，我的孩子；让我带了你去罢。"

我便要回答道："你没有看见么，叔父，我已是同父亲一样大了。我决定要独自一个人到市场里去。"

叔父便将说道："是的，他随便要到哪里去都可以，因为他是大人了。"

当我正把钱给我乳娘时，母亲便要从浴室中出来，因为我是知道怎样用我的钥匙去开银箱的。

① slate [sleit] *n.*（书写用的）画石板

give silver to my nurse."

Mother will say to herself, "He can give money to whom he likes, for he is grown up."

In the holiday time in October father will come home and, thinking that I am still a baby, will bring for me from the town little shoes and small **silken**[①] frocks.

I shall say, "Father, give them to my dādā, for I am as big as you are."

Father will think and say, "He can buy his own clothes if he likes, for he is grown up."

母亲将要说道:"你做什么呀,坏孩子?"

我便要告诉她道:"母亲,你不知道,我已是同父亲一样大了,我必须给钱给乳娘。"

母亲便将自语道:"他可以随便把钱给他所喜欢给的人,因为他是大人了。"

当十月里放假的时候,父亲将要回家,他以为我还是一个孩子,还为我从城里带了小鞋子,小绸衫来。

我便要说道:"父亲,把这些东西给了哥哥罢,因为我已是同你一样大了。"

父亲便将想了一想,说道:"他可以随便去买他自己穿的衣裳,因为他是大人了。"

① silken ['silkən] *a.* 丝绸做的

# Twelve O'clock

Mother, I do want to leave off my lessons now. I have been at my book all the morning.

You say it is only twelve o'clock. Suppose it isn't any later; can't you ever think it is afternoon when it is only twelve o'clock?

I can easily imagine now that the sun has reached the edge of that rice-field, and the old fisher-woman is gathering **herbs**[①] for her supper by the side of the pond.

I can just shut my eyes and think that the shadows are growing darker under the *madar*[②] tree, and the water in the pond looks shiny black.

If twelve o'clock can come in the night, why can't the night come when it is twelve o'clock?

# 十二点钟

妈妈，我真想现在不做功课了。我整个早晨都在念书呢。

你说，现在还不过是十二点钟。假定不会晚过十二点罢；难道你不能把不过是十二点钟想象成下午么？

我能够容容易易地想象：现在太阳已经到了那片稻田的边缘上了，老态龙钟的渔婆正在池边采撷香草做她的晚餐。

我闭上了眼就能够想到，马塔尔树下的阴影是更深黑了，池塘里的水看来黑得发亮。

假如十二点钟能够在黑夜里来到，为什么黑夜不能在十二点钟的时候来到呢？

① herb [hə:b] *n.* （用作食品的）香草

② madar〈印〉马塔尔树

# Authorship

You say that father writes a lot of books, but what he writes I don't understand.

He was reading to you all the evening, but could you really **make out**[1] what he meant?

What nice stories, mother, you can tell us! Why can't father write like that, I wonder?

Did he never hear from his own mother stories of giants and fairies and princesses?

Has he forgotten them all?

Often when he gets late for his bath you have to go and call him a hundred times.

You wait and keep his dishes warm for him, but he goes on writing and forgets.

Father always plays at making books.

If ever I go to play in father's room, you come and call me, "What a naughty child!"

If I make the slightest noise, you say, "Don't you see that father's at his work?"

# 著作家

你说父亲写了许多书，但我却不懂他所写的是什么。

他整个黄昏把书读给你听，但是你真能懂得他的意义么？

母亲，你讲给我们的故事，真是好听呀！我很奇怪父亲为什么不能写像那样的书呢？

难道他始终没有从他自己的母亲那里听见过巨人和神仙和公主的故事么？

还是已把他们全忘记了？

常常的，当他要沐浴时，总是耽搁着，你总要走去叫他一百多次。

你总要等候着，把他的菜温着等他，但他忘了，还尽管写下去。

父亲常常以著书为游戏。

如果我一走进父亲房里去游戏，你就要来叫道："真是一个坏孩子！"

如果我轻轻地响了一下，你就要说："你没有看见你父亲正在工作么？"

① make out 理解

What's the fun of always writing and writing?

When I take up father's pen or pencil and write upon his book just as he does, — a, b, c, d, e, f, g, h, i, — why do you **get cross with**① me, then, mother?

You never say a word when father writes.

When my father wastes such heaps of paper, mother, you don't seem to mind at all.

But if I take only one sheet to make a boat with, you say, "Child, how **trouble-some**② you are!"

What do you think of father's spoiling sheets and sheets of paper with black marks all over on both sides?

① get cross with [口语]
　对……发脾气，对……
　生气

② trouble-some ['trʌblsəm]
　*a.* 使人恼火的

常常地写了又写，有什么趣味呢？

当我拿起父亲的笔或铅笔，像他一模一样地在他书上写着，——a，b，c，d，e，f，g，h，i，——那时你为什么阻拦着我写呢，母亲？

父亲写时，你却不说一句话。

当我父亲耗费了那许多纸时，母亲，你似乎全不在意。

如果我只取了一张纸去做一只船，你却要说："孩子，你真是淘气！"

你对于父亲拿黑点子涂满了纸的两面．污损了许多许多张纸，你心里以为怎样呢？

# The Wicked&#9312; Postman

Why do you sit there on the floor so quiet and silent, tell me, mother dear?

The rain is coming in through the open window, making you all wet, and you don't mind it.

Do you hear the gong striking four? It is time for my brother to come home from school.

What has happened to you that you look so strange?

Haven't you got a letter from father today?

I saw the postman bringing letters in his bag for almost everybody in the town.

Only, father's letters he keeps to read himself. I am sure the postman is a wicked man.

But don't be unhappy about that, mother dear.

To-morrow is market day in the next village. You ask your **maid**&#9313; to buy some pens and papers.

I myself will write all father's letters; you will not find a single mistake.

I shall write from A **right up**&#9314; to K.

But, mother, why do you smile?

You don't believe that I can write as nicely as father does!

# 恶邮差

① wicked ['wikid] *a.* 坏的

你为什么坐在那边地板上不言不动的，告诉我呀，亲爱的母亲？

雨从开着的窗口打进来了，你身上全湿了，你却不管。

你听见钟已打了四下么？正是哥哥从学校里回家的时候了。

到底发生了什么事，你为什么神色这样不对？

你今天没有接到父亲的信么？

我看见邮差在他袋里带了许多的信来，几乎镇里的每个人都分送到了。

只有，只有父亲的信，他要藏起来给他自己读。我敢决定这个邮差是个坏人。

但是不要因此不乐呀，亲爱的母亲。

② maid [meid] *n.* 女仆

明天是邻村市集的日子。你叫女仆去买些笔与纸来。

我自己会写一切父亲所写的信；使你找不出一点错处来。

③ right up 直到

我要从 A 字一直写到 K 字。

但是，母亲，你为什么笑呢？

But I shall **rule**① my paper carefully, and write all the letters beautifully big.

When I finish my writing, do you think I shall be so foolish as father and drop it into the horrid postman's bag?

I shall bring it to you myself without waiting, and letter by letter help you to read my writing.

I know the postman does not like to give you the really nice letters.

① rule [ru:l] *v.* ( 用尺等 )
在……上画线

你不相信我能写得同父亲一样好!

但是我将用心画纸格,把所有的字母都大大地美丽地写出来。

当我写好了时,你以为我也像父亲那样傻,把它投入可怕的邮差的袋中么?

我立刻就自己送来给你,还一个字母,一个字母地帮助你读。

我知道那邮差是不肯把真正的好信送给你的。

# The Hero

Mother, let us imagine we are travelling and passing through a strange and dangerous country.

You are riding in a **palanquin**① and I am **trotting**② by you on a red horse.

It is evening and the sun goes down. The waste of *Joradighi*③ lies **wan**④ and grey before us. The land is desolate and **barren**⑤.

You are frightened and thinking—"I know not where we have come to."

I say to you, "Mother, do not be afraid."

The meadow is **prickly**⑥ with **spiky**⑦ grass, and through it runs a narrow broken path.

There are no cattle to be seen in the wide field; they have gone to their village stalls.

It grows dark and dim on the land and sky, and we cannot tell where we are going.

Suddenly you call me and ask me in a whisper, "What light is that near the bank?"

Just then there bursts out a fearful yell, and figures come running towards us.

# 英雄

① palanquin [ˌpælən'kiːn] n.
（旧时东亚国家两人或
更多人抬的）轿子

② trot [trɔt] v. 骑马小跑

③ Joradighi〈印〉约拉地
希

④ wan [wɔn] a. 无力的

⑤ barren ['bærən] a.（土
地）贫瘠的，荒芜的

⑥ prickly ['prikli] a. 多刺
的

⑦ spiky ['spaiki] a. 长而尖
的

妈妈，让我们想象我们正在旅行，经过一个陌生而危险的国土。

你坐在一顶轿子里，我骑着一匹红马，在你旁边跑着。

是黄昏的时候，太阳已经下山了。约拉地希的荒地疲乏而灰暗地展开在我们面前，大地是凄凉而荒芜的。

你害怕了，想道——"我不知道我们到了什么地方了。"

我对你说道："妈妈，不要害怕。"

草地上刺蓬蓬地长着针尖似的草，一条狭而崎岖的小道通过这块草地。

在这片广大的地面上看不见一只牛；它们已经回到它们村里的牛棚去了。

天色黑了下来，大地和天空都显得朦朦胧胧的，而我们不能说出我们正走向什么所在。

突然间，你叫我，悄悄地问我："靠近河岸的是什么火光呀？"

正在那个时候，一阵可怕的呐喊声爆发了，好些人影子向我们跑过来。

You sit **crouched**① in your palanquin and repeat the names of the gods in prayer.

The **bearers**②, shaking in terror, hide themselves in the **thorny**③ bush.

I shout to you, "Don't be afraid, mother, I am here."

With long sticks in their hands and hair all wild about their heads, they come nearer and nearer.

I shout, "Have a care! You **villains**④! One step more and you are dead men."

They give another terrible yell and rush forward.

You clutch my hand and say, "Dear boy, for heaven's sake, keep away from them."

I say, "Mother, just you watch me."

Then I **spur**⑤ my horse for a wild **gallop**⑥, and my sword and **buckler**⑦ clash against each other.

The fight becomes so fearful, mother, that it would give you a cold shudder could you see it from your palanquin.

Many of them fly, and a great number are cut to pieces.

I know you are thinking, sitting all by yourself, that your boy must be dead by this time.

But I come to you all stained with blood, and say, "Mother, the fight is over now."

You come out and kiss me, pressing me to your heart, and you say to yourself,

"I don't know what I should do if I hadn't my boy to **escort**⑧ me."

A thousand useless things happen day after day, and why couldn't such a thing come true by chance?

It would be like a story in a book.

① crouch [krautʃ] v. 蹲

② bearer [ˈbɛərə] n. 轿夫
③ thorny [ˈθɔːni] a. 荆棘丛
生的

④ villain [ˈvilən] n. 恶棍

⑤ spur [spə:] v.（用踢马
刺）策（马）
⑥ gallop [ˈgæləp] n. 骑马奔
驰
⑦ buckler [ˈbʌklə] n. 盾牌，
小圆盾

⑧ escort [ˈeskɔ:t] v. 护卫，
护送

你蹲坐在你的轿子里，嘴里反复地祷念着神的名字。

轿夫们怕得发抖，躲藏在荆棘丛中。

我向你喊道："不要害怕，妈妈，有我在这里。"

他们手里执着长棒，头发披散着，越走越近了。

我喊道："要当心！你们这些坏蛋！再向前走一步，你们就要送命了。"

他们又发出一阵可怕的呐喊声，向前冲过来。

你抓住我的手，说道："好孩子，看在上天面上，躲开他们罢。"

我说道："妈妈，你瞧我的。"

于是我刺策着我的马匹，猛奔过去，我的剑和盾彼此碰着作响。

这一场战斗是那么激烈，妈妈，如果你从轿子里看得见的话，你一定会发冷战的。

他们之中，许多人逃走了，还有好些人被砍杀了。

我知道你那时独自坐在那里，心里正在想着，你的孩子这时候一定已经死了。

但是我跑到你的跟前，浑身溅满了鲜血．说道："妈妈，现在战争已经结束了。"

你从轿子里走出来，吻着我，把我搂在你的心头，你自言自语地说道：

"如果我没有我的孩子护送我，我简直不知道怎么办才好。"

一千件无聊的事天天在发生，为什么这样一件事不能够偶然实现呢？

这很像一本书里的一个故事。

My brother would say, "Is it possible? I always thought he was so **delicate**[①]!"

Our village people would all say in amazement, "Was it not lucky that the boy was with his mother?"

① delicate ['delikət] *a.* 娇弱的

　　我的哥哥要说道："这是可能的事么？我老是在想，他是那么嫩弱呢！"

　　我们村里的人们都要惊讶地说："这孩子正和他妈妈在一起，这不是很幸运么？"

# The End

It is time for me to go, mother; I am going.

When in the **paling**① darkness of the lonely dawn you stretch out your arms for your baby in the bed, I shall say, "Baby is not there!"—mother, I am going.

I shall become a delicate **draught**② of air and **caress**③ you; and I shall be **ripples**④ in the water when you bathe, and kiss you and kiss you again.

In the **gusty**⑤ night when the rain patters on the leaves you will hear my whisper in your bed, and my laughter will flash with the lightning through the open window into your room.

If you lie awake, thinking of your baby till late into the night, I shall sing to you from the stars, "Sleep, mother, sleep."

On the **straying**⑥ moonbeams I shall steal over your bed, and lie upon your bosom while you sleep.

I shall become a dream, and through the little opening of your eyelids I shall slip into the depths of your sleep, and when you wake up and look round **startled**⑦, like a twinkling firefly I shall flit out into the darkness.

# 告别

是我走的时候了，母亲；我走了。

当清寂的黎明，你在暗中，伸出双臂，要抱你睡在床上的孩子时，我要说道："孩子不在那里呀！"——母亲，我走了。

我要变成一股清风抚摸着你，我要变成水中的小波，当你浴时把你吻了又吻。

大风之夜，当雨点在树叶中淅沥时，你在床上，会听见我的微语，当电光从开着的窗口闪进你的屋里时，我的笑声也偕了它一同闪进了。

如果你醒着躺在床上，想着你的孩子到了深夜，我便要从群星里向你唱道："睡呀，母亲，睡呀。"

我要坐在照澈各处的月光上，偷到你的床上，乘你睡着时，躺在你的胸上。

我要变成一个梦儿，从你眼皮的小孔中，钻到你睡眠的深处；当你醒起来吃惊地四看时，我便如闪耀的萤火似的熠熠地向暗中飞去了。

① paling ['peiliŋ] v.（pale 的现在分词）变得苍白，变得暗淡
② draught [drɑ:ft] n. 气流
③ caress [kə'res] v. 抚摸，轻抚
④ ripple ['ripl] n. 微波，涟漪
⑤ gusty ['gʌsti] a.（风）阵阵劲吹的

⑥ straying [streiŋ] v.（stray 的现在分词）游荡

⑦ startled ['stɑ:tld] v.（startle 的过去分词）吃惊

When, on the great festival of ***puja***①, the neighbours' children come and play about the house, I shall melt into the music of the flute and **throb**② in your heart all day.

Dear auntie will come with *puja*-presents and will ask, "Where is our baby, sister?" Mother, you will tell her softly, "He is in the **pupils**③ of my eyes, he is in my body and in my soul."

① puja [ˈpuːdʒɑː] *n.* 印度教
的礼拜

② throb [θrɔb] *v.* 震颤，震
动

③ pupil [ˈpjuːpəl] *n.*【解剖
学】瞳孔

当普耶大祭日[1]，邻家的孩子们来屋里游玩时，我便要融化在笛声里，整日价在你心头震荡。

亲爱的阿姨带了普耶礼[2]来，问道："我的孩子在哪里呢，姊姊？"母亲，你要柔声地告诉她："他呀，他现在是在我的瞳人[3]里，他现在是在我的身体里，在我的灵魂里。"

---

1　普耶原文为 Puja，同 Pooja，梵语"崇拜"，印度人对于典礼的崇拜都叫 Puja，并无一定的节。这里所谓"普耶大祭日"是随意指印度的某一个大祭神日。

2　普耶礼就是指某一个节日亲友相互馈送的礼物。

3　现在一般写作"瞳仁"。

# The Recall

The night was dark when she went away, and they slept.

The night is dark now, and I call for her, "Come back, my darling; the world is asleep; and no one would know, if you come for a moment while stars are gazing at stars."

She went away when the trees were in bud and the spring was young.

Now the flowers are in high bloom and I call, "Come back, my darling. The children gather and scatter flowers in **reckless**① sport. And if you come and take one little blossom no one will miss it."

Those that used to play are playing still, so **spendthrift**② is life.

I listen to their chatter and call, "Come back, my darling, for mother's heart is full to the **brim**③ with love, and if you come to snatch only one little kiss from her no one will **grudge**④ it."

# 追唤

她走的时候，夜间黑漆漆的，他们都睡了。

现在，夜间也是黑漆漆的，我唤她道："回来，我爱；世界都在沉睡；当群星互相凝视的时候，你来一会儿是没有人知道的。"

她走的时候，树木刚在萌芽，春光正幼。

现在花盛开了，我唤道："回来，我爱。孩子们漫不经心地游戏，把花聚了一块，又把它们散开了。你如走来，拿一朵小花去，没有人会觉得失了它的。"

他们常常游戏的，还在那里游戏，生命如此的浪费。

我静听他们的空谈，便唤道："回来，我爱，母亲的心里，充满着爱，你如走来，仅从她那里接了一个吻，没有人会妒忌的。"

① reckless ['reklis] a. 不在意的

② spendthrift ['spendθrift] a. 挥霍的，浪费的
③ brim [brim] n. 边缘
④ grudge [grʌdʒ] v. 妒忌

# The First Jasmines<sup>①</sup>

Ah, these jasmines, these white jasmines!

I seem to remember the first day when I filled my hands with these jasmines, these white jasmines.

I have loved the sunlight, the sky and the green earth;

I have heard the liquid murmur of the river through the darkness of midnight;

Autumn sunsets have come to me at the bend of a road in the lonely waste, like a bride raising her **veil**<sup>②</sup> to accept her lover.

Yet my memory is still sweet with the first white jasmines that I held in my hand when I was a child.

Many a glad day has come in my life, and I have laughed with **merrymakers**<sup>③</sup> on festival nights.

On grey mornings of rain I have **crooned**<sup>④</sup> many an idle song.

I have worn round my neck the evening **wreath**<sup>⑤</sup> of *bakulas* woven by the hand of love.

Yet my heart is sweet with the memory of the first fresh jasmines that filled my hands when I was a child.

# 第一次的茉莉

① jasmine ['dʒæsmin] *n.*
【植物】茉莉

呵，这些茉莉花，这些白的茉莉花！

我似乎忆起我第一次双手满捧着这些茉莉花，这些白的茉莉花的时候。

我喜欢那日光，那天空，那绿色的大地；

我听见那河水淙净的流声，在黑漆的中夜里传过来；

② veil [veil] *n.* 面纱

我看见那秋天的夕阳，在荒野的路角，映照在我的身上，如新妇揭起她的面网迎接她的爱人。

但我想起孩提时第一次捧在手里的白茉莉，心里还感着甜蜜的回忆。

③ merrymaker
['meri,meikə] *n.* 狂欢者

我生平有过许多快活的日子，在宴会的晚上，我跟了说笑话的人而大笑。

④ croon [kru:n] *v.* 低吟

在灰暗的雨晨，我吟哦着许多飘逸的诗篇。

⑤ wreath [ri:θ] *n.* 花环

我头上戴过爱人手织的夜晚的醉花的花圈。

但我想起孩提时第一次捧在手里的白茉莉，心里还感着甜蜜的回忆。

# The Banyan Tree

O you **shaggy**①-headed banyan tree standing on the bank of the pond, have you forgotten the little child, like the birds that have nested in your branches and left you?

Do you not remember how he sat at the window and wondered at the tangle of your roots that **plunged**② underground?

The women would come to fill their jars in the pond, and your huge black shadow would **wriggle**③ on the water like sleep struggling to wake up.

Sunlight danced on the ripples like restless tiny **shuttles**④ weaving golden **tapestry**⑤.

Two ducks swam by the weedy margin above their shadows, and the child would sit still and think.

He longed to be the wind and blow through your rustling branches, to be your shadow and lengthen with the day on the water, to be a bird and **perch**⑥ on your topmost twig, and to float like those ducks among the weeds and shadows.

# 榕树

① shaggy ['ʃægi] *a.* 蓬乱的

② plunge [plʌndʒ] *v.* 投入，插入

③ wriggle ['rigl] *v.* 扭动
④ shuttle ['ʃʌtl] *n.* 梭
⑤ tapestry ['tæpistri] *n.* 织锦

⑥ perch [pəːtʃ] *v.* 栖息

喂，你站在池边的蓬头榕树，你可会忘记了那孩子，那像巢于你的枝上又离了你的鸟儿似的孩子？

你不记得他怎样坐在窗内，诧望着你伸在地下的纠缠的树根么？

妇人们常到池边，汲了满瓶的水去．你的大黑影便在水面上摇动，好像睡着的人挣扎着要醒来似的。

日光在微波上跳舞，好像不停不息的小梭在金丝的缎布机上穿来穿去。

两只鸭子旁着¹芦苇边游着，在它们的影子上，游来游去，孩子静静地坐在那里想着。

他想做风，吹过你的萧萧的枝杈中；想做你的影子，在水面上，随了日光而俱长；想做一只鸟儿，栖息在你的最高枝上；还想像那两只鸭，在芦苇与荫影中间游来游去。

---

1　现在一般写作"傍着"。

# Benediction[①]

Bless this little heart, this white soul that has won the kiss of heaven for our earth.

He loves the light of the sun, he loves the sight of his mother's face.

He has not learned to **despise**[②] the dust, and to **hanker after**[③] gold.

Clasp him to your heart and bless him.

He has come into this land of a hundred cross-roads.

I know not how he chose you from the crowd, came to your door, and grasped your hand to ask his way.

He will follow you, laughing and talking and not a doubt in his heart.

Keep his trust, lead him straight and bless him.

Lay your hand on his head, and pray that though the waves underneath grow threatening, yet the breath from above may come and fill his sails and **waft**[④] him to the haven of peace.

Forget him not in your hurry, let him come to your heart and bless him.

# 祝福

① benediction [ˌbeniˈdikʃən]
  *n.* 祝福

② despise [diˈspaiz] *v.* 鄙
  视，看不起
③ hanker after 渴望

④ waft [wɑ:ft] *v.* 吹送

祝福这个小心灵，这个洁白的灵魂，他为我们的大地，赢得了天的接吻。

他爱日光，他爱见他母亲的脸。

他没有学别人之侮蔑尘土，以寻求黄金。

紧抱他在你心里，祝福他。

他已来到这个歧路百出的地上了。

我不知道他怎样要从群众中选出你来，来到你的门前，握着你的手，访问他的路程。

他笑着，谈着，跟着你走，心里没有一点儿疑惑。

保守着他的信任，引导他到正路，祝福他。

把你的手摆在头上，祈求着：底下的波涛虽恶，然而从上面来的风，会吹拂来，而吸饱他的船帆，送他到和平的港口的。

在你的忙碌里，不要忘了他，让他来到你的心里，并且祝福他。

# The Gift

I want to give you something, my child, for we are drifting in the stream of the world.

Our lives will be carried apart, and our love forgotten.

But I am not so foolish as to hope that I could buy your heart with my gifts.

Young is your life, your path long, and you drink the love we bring you at one **draught**① and turn and run away from us.

You have your play and your playmates. What harm is there if you have no time or thought for us?

We, indeed, have leisure enough in old age to count the days that are past, to cherish in our hearts what our hands have lost for ever.

The river runs swift with a song, breaking through all barriers. But the mountain stays and remembers, and follows her with his love.

# 赠品

我要送些东西给你，我的孩子，因为我们同是漂泊在世界的溪流中的。

我们的生命将被隔离了，我们的爱也将被忘记。

但我却没有那样傻，希望我能用我的赠品来买你的心。

你的生命正是青春，你的道路也长着呢，你一口气饮了我们带给你的爱，便回身离开我们跑了。

你有你的游戏，有你的游伴。如果你没有时间同我们游戏，如果你想不到我们，那是没有什么关系的。

我们呢，自然的，在老年时，会有许多闲暇的时间，去数那过去的日子，把我们手里永久失了的东西，在心里抚摸着。

河流唱着歌很快地流去，冲破所有的堤防。但是山峰却停留着，记念着，含情送了她去。

① draught [drɑ:ft] *n.* 一饮

# My Song

This song of mine will **wind** its music **around**① you, my child, like the **fond**② arms of love.

This song of mine will touch your forehead like a kiss of blessing.

When you are alone it will sit by your side and whisper in your ear, when you are in the crowd it will **fence** you **about**③ with **aloofness**④.

My song will be like a pair of wings to your dreams, it will transport your heart to the **verge**⑤ of the unknown.

It will be like the faithful star overhead when dark night is over your road.

My song will sit in the pupils of your eyes, and will carry your sight into the heart of things.

And when my voice is silent in death, my song will speak in your living heart.

# 我的歌

① wind around 把……绕在……周围
② fond [fɔnd] *a.* 充满深情的，柔情的

③ fence about 保护
④ aloofness [əˈluːfnis] *n.* 远离

⑤ verge [vəːdʒ] *n.* 边，边缘

　　我的小孩呀，我这一支歌将扬起它的乐声围绕你的身旁，好像那爱的热恋的手臂一样。我这一支歌将接触着你的前额，好像那祝福的接吻一样。

　　当你只是一个人的时候，它将坐在你的身边，在你耳旁微语，当你在人群中的时候，它将远远地围着你保护着你。

　　我的歌又好像一双属于你梦境的羽翼，它将把你的心移送到不可知的岸上去。

　　当黑夜覆盖在你路上的时候，它又像那照临在你头上的忠实的星光一样。

　　我的歌又将坐在你眼睛的瞳人里，将你的视线带入万物的心里。

　　我的歌声虽因死而沉寂，但是我的歌仍将从你活泼泼的心中唱将出来。

# The Child-Angel

They **clamour**① and fight, they doubt and despair, they know no end to their **wranglings**②.

Let your life come amongst them like a flame of light, my child, unflickering and pure, and delight them into silence.

They are cruel in their greed and their envy, their words are like hidden knives thirsting for blood.

Go and stand amidst their scowling hearts, my child, and let your gentle eyes fall upon them like the forgiving peace of the evening over the **strife**③ of the day.

Let them see your face, my child, and thus know the meaning of all things; let them love you and thus love each other.

Come and take your seat in the bosom of the limitless, my child. At sunrise open and raise your heart like a blossoming flower, and at sunset bend your head and in silence complete the worship of the day.

# 孩提之天使

① clamour ['klæmə] v. 大嚷
大叫
② wrangling ['ræŋgliŋ] v.
（wrangle 的现在分词）
争吵

③ strife [straif] n. 冲突

他们喧哗争斗，他们怀疑失望，他们辩论而不知结果。

我的孩子，让你的生命到他们当中去．如一线镇定而纯洁之光，使他们愉悦而沉默。

当他们贪望妒忌的时候，是残忍的；他们的话，好像藏着的刀，渴欲饮血。

我的孩子，去，去立在他们黑漆漆的心中，把你的和善的眼光堕在他们上面，好像那傍晚的慈善的和平，覆盖着日间的骚扰一样。

我的孩子，让他们看你的脸，因此能够知道一切事的意义；让他们爱你，因此使他们相爱。

来，坐在"无限"的底上，我的孩子，在朝阳出时，开放而抬起你的心像一朵开着的花，在夕阳落时，低下你的头，沉默地完成了日间之崇拜。

# The Last Bargain<sup>①</sup>

"Come and hire me," I cried, while in the morning I was walking on the stone-paved road.

Sword in hand, the King came in his **chariot**②.

He held my hand and said, "I will hire you with my power."

But his power counted for **nought**③, and he went away in his chariot.

In the heat of the midday the houses stood with shut doors.

I wandered along the **crooked**④ lane.

An old man came out with his bag of gold.

He **pondered**⑤ and said, "I will hire you with my money."

He weighed his coins one by one, but I turned away.

It was evening. The garden **hedge**⑥ was all aflower.

The fair maid came out and said, "I will hire you with a smile."

Her smile paled and melted into tears, and she went back alone into the dark.

The sun glistened on the sand, and the sea waves broke **waywardly**⑦.

A child sat playing with shells.

# 最后的契约

① bargain ['bɑ:gin] *n.* 契约

② chariot ['tʃæriət] *n.* [古语] 轻便四轮马车（供游览或隆重场合用）

③ nought [nɔ:t] *n.* (=naught) 无足轻重的人（或东西）

④ crooked ['krukid] *a.* 弯曲的

⑤ ponder ['pɔndə] *v.* 考虑

⑥ hedge [hedʒ] *n.* (矮树) 树篱，（树枝等的）篱笆

⑦ waywardly ['weiwədli] *ad.* 刚愎自用地，任性地

早晨，我在石铺的路上走时，我叫道："来雇我。"

皇帝坐着马车，手里拿着剑走来。

他拿住我的手，说道："我要用权力来雇你。"

但是他的权力算不了什么，他坐着马车走了。

正午炎热的时候，家家的门都闭着。

我沿着屈曲的小道走去。

一个老人带着一袋金钱走出来。

他斟酌了一下，说道："我要用金钱来雇你。"

他一个一个地称量他的钱，但我却转身离去了。

黄昏的时候，花园的篱上满开着花。

美人走出来，说道："我要用微笑来雇你。"

她的微笑灰白了，融化成眼泪了，她孤寂地回身走进黑暗里去。

太阳照耀在沙土上，海波刚愎地碎开了。

一个小孩坐在那里，拿贝壳做游戏。

He raised his head and seemed to know me, and said, "I hire you with nothing."

From thenceforward that bargain struck[①] in child's play made me a free man.

他抬起头来，好像认识我似的，说道："我雇你不用什么东西。"

这个小孩的游戏中的买卖，使我从此以后，成了一个自由的人。

① struck [strʌk] v. ( strike 的过去分词 ) 达成